Dear Parents,

ASPCA Rescue Readers series tells stories of animal adventures from the animal's point of view! Written with warmth and gentle humor, these leveled texts are designed to support young readers in their growth while connecting to their passion for pets.

Level 2 in this series is designed for early readers who need short, simple sentences, familiar vocabulary, informative illustrations, and easier spelling patterns to give them support as they practice to become fluent readers.

When you're reading with your children, you can help by encouraging them to think about using more than one strategy to unlock new words. Successful readers solve words in a variety of ways. Here are some tips you might share with your child:

- Take a picture walk before you read so you can preview the story.

- Sound out the word, remembering that some letters say more than one sound.

- For long words, cover up the end so you can figure out the beginning first.

- Check the picture to see if it gives you some clues.

- Skip over the word and read a little further along. Then come back to it.

- Think about what is happening in this story. What would make sense here?

Learning to read is an exciting time in a child's life. A wonderful way to share in that time is to have conversations about the books after reading. Children love talking about their favorite part, or connecting the story to their own lives. I hope you'll enjoy sharing in the fun as your children get to know Picasso and all the other adopted pets that are part of this series. Happy reading!

Ellie Costa, M.S. Ed.
Literacy Specialist, Bank Street College of Education

Published by Studio Fun International, Inc.
44 South Broadway, White Plains, NY 10601 U.S.A. and
Studio Fun International Limited,
The Ice House, 124-126 Walcot Street, Bath UK BA1 5BG
Illustration © 2015 Studio Fun International, Inc.
Text © 2015 ASPCA®
All rights reserved.
Studio Fun Books is a trademark of Studio Fun International, Inc.,
a subsidiary of The Reader's Digest Association, Inc.
Printed in China.
Conforms to ASTM F963
10 9 8 7 6 5 4 3 2 1
SL2/05/15
Cover photo © ryasick/iphoto.com

*The American Society for the Prevention of Cruelty to Animals (ASPCA®) will
receive a minimum guarantee from Studio Fun International, Inc. of $25,000
for the sale of ASPCA® products through December 2017.
Comments? Questions? Call us at: 1-800-217-3346

Library of Congress Control Number: 2015939443

I Am Picasso

written by
Picasso

(with help from Lori C. Froeb)

illustrated by Deborah Melmon

studio fun

A READER'S DIGEST COMPANY

White Plains, New York • Montréal, Québec • Bath, United Kingdom

Woof! Woof!

I am Picasso!

I am a little puppy
that lives in a big house.

Look at my things!

I have a blue bowl.

I have a red leash and harness.

This is my bed.

Tori made it for me.

Do you want to meet Tori?

Let's find her!

I found her!

Tori is in my favorite room!

It is the art room.

Tori and Dad like to paint.

Dad is painting right now!

Look at all the art!

I know I belong with Tori and Dad.
Look! We have the same hair!

We met at the shelter.
There were five puppies.
They picked me!

My first day home was great.
I ate yummy food.

I played with Tori.
She brushed my fur.

Then she gave me my name.

It is Picasso.

She said Picasso is

her favorite painter.

Painting looks fun.
I want to see
what Dad is painting!

Woof! Woof! Woof!

What are you painting, Dad?

Uh-oh.

I made a mess.

Dad and Tori want to play!
I play tag.
They can't catch me!

Whoops!

Dad's art is on the floor.

Woof! Woof!

Tag is fun!

The paint is cold and wet.
Look at all the colors!

Red. Blue. Pink. Green.

Green! I like green.

Look at my paw prints.

I can make art, too!

Tori shouts my name.
"Picasso! Picasso, sit."
I sit. I am tired.

Tori gives me a hug.

Dad does not look happy.

Woof! I made art!

"Dad! Look at Picasso's art!"
Tori says.
"It looks like your art!"

Dad smiles.

He says I'm an artist, too!

Just like Picasso.

Now, I have my own paint.
I make my own art.
Red. Blue. Pink. Green.
Green. I like green.

We make art together.
Dad and Tori put my art
up on the wall, too.

Dad has an art show.

I have an art show, too.

People shake Dad's hand.

They pat my head.

"This pup can paint!"
a nice lady says.

27

The lady buys my painting.

Tori says I am a star.

I feel like a star.

I sign the painting
with a paw print.
It is green.

I am Picasso
and I like to paint—
just like Tori and
just like Dad.

31

Meet a real ASPCA rescue:
Mikey

Mikey was found wandering the streets
of Brooklyn, New York. He didn't look like he
does here. He was dirty and his hair was so
matted, he could barely see through the thick
tangles. A kind person brought him to a rescue
where the volunteers fed him, washed him,
and worked with him for over a month to get
him ready for adoption. Finally, he found
his forever home with Emily and now has a
four-legged sister, Olive!

For more information on how to help animals,
go to **www.aspca.org/parents**.